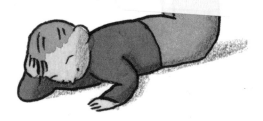

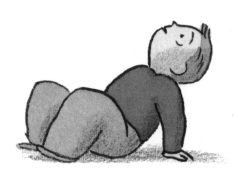

A big fat kiss to Joanna Cotler, and a thank you to
Jean de Brunhoff for my utopia: Celesteville.

—M.R.

Library of Congress Cataloging-in-Publication Data

Rosenthal, Marc.

Phooey! / Marc Rosenthal.— 1st ed.

p.   cm.

Summary: A boy who claims there is nothing to do spends his day being anything but bored.

ISBN-10: 0-06-075248-3 (trade bdg.) — ISBN-13: 978-0-06-075248-4 (trade bdg.)

ISBN-10: 0-06-075249-1 (lib. bdg.) — ISBN-13: 978-0-06-075249-1 (lib. bdg.)

[1. Boredom—Fiction. 2. Humorous stories.] I. Title.

PZ7.R719446Pho 2007   2006020218

[E]—dc22   CIP

                                                                    AC

Typography by Neil Swaab 1 2 3 4 5 6 7 8 9 10 ❖ First Edition

PHOOEY!

by Marc Rosenthal

Joanna Cotler Books
An Imprint of HarperCollinsPublishers

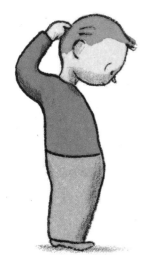